W9-AWH-671

MR. BUTTERBY'S
AMAZING MACHINES

Written by Pauline Cartwright
Illustrated by Philip Webb

Mr. Butterby wanted to fly.
He was always in his shed
inventing amazing machines.

"Come and watch me, my dear,"
he would call to his wife.
"This one will work!"
But not one of his amazing machines ever did.

One day, Mr. Butterby made wings
with real feathers.
He tried to fly around the backyard.
Crash!
"You should invent a *useful* machine,"
Mrs. Butterby told him crossly.
She left him untangling his wings,
and went off to do her shopping.
"Watch the house while I'm gone,"
she called.

CRASH!!

Mr. Butterby went back to his shed.
He had a new idea about how to fly.
He was so busy with his new idea,
he didn't hear the robber.

"Oh, really, Mr. Butterby!"
said Mrs. Butterby.
"You should have been watching the house.
I do wish you were more *useful*.
The robber has taken my best silver spoons."

The next day, Mr. Butterby said he would stay
in the house while Mrs. Butterby played golf.
Another idea popped into his head.
"I can invent machines.
I'll invent a robber-catching machine!
A robber-catching machine is a very *useful* machine.
It will give Mrs. Butterby a big surprise."

When he had finished making his new machine,
Mr. Butterby stood back admiring it.
"No robbers will get into our house now,"
he said.
While he waited for his wife,
he went to sleep in the chair.
He didn't hear Mrs. Butterby come home.

The robber-catching machine
gave Mrs. Butterby a VERY BIG surprise!
She yelled in fright,
and Mr. Butterby woke from his sleep.
"The robber! I've caught the robber!
I wish my dear wife was here to see this!"
said Mr. Butterby.

"I AM here!"
said Mrs. Butterby.
"Oh, my dear, it's you!" he cried in shock.
Mrs. Butterby looked very upset.
Mr. Butterby was very upset too.

"The next time I play golf
I shall lock up the house,"
she said to Mr. Butterby.
"Then you can stay in your shed.
So never mind about inventing
any more *useful* machines."

But right away, a new idea for a machine
popped into Mr. Butterby's head.

He went off to his shed
to make another amazing machine.
Maybe this one would work.
Maybe . . . .

THE
HIGHGATE
COLLECTION

United States edition published in 1991 by
Steck-Vaughn Company
P.O. Box 26015
Austin, Texas 78755.
Steck-Vaughn Company is a subsidiary
of National Education Corporation.

First published in 1989 in New Zealand by
Nelson Price Milburn Ltd.
1 Te Puni Street, Petone

Mr. Butterby's Amazing Machines
ISBN   0 8114 2690 4
Text © Pauline Cartwright
Illustrations © Nelson Price Milburn Ltd.
© 1990 Nelson Price Milburn Ltd.

Printed in Hong Kong.

Library of Congress Cataloging-in-Publication Data: Cartwright, Pauline, 1944– / Mr. Butterby's
amazing machines / written by Pauline Cartwright; illustrated by Philip Webb.
p. cm. — (Highgate collection)
"Published in New Zealand by Nelson Price Milburn Ltd. ... Petone" — Verso t.p. SUMMARY: Mr.
Butterby's useless inventions annoy his wife, especially the robber-catching machine that catches
her instead.
ISBN 0-8114-2690-4
[1. Invention — Fiction.] I. Webb, Philip, ill. II. Title. III. Series. PZ7.C2517Mr 1990 [Fic]—dc20
90–10072   CIP   AC